But I love You more

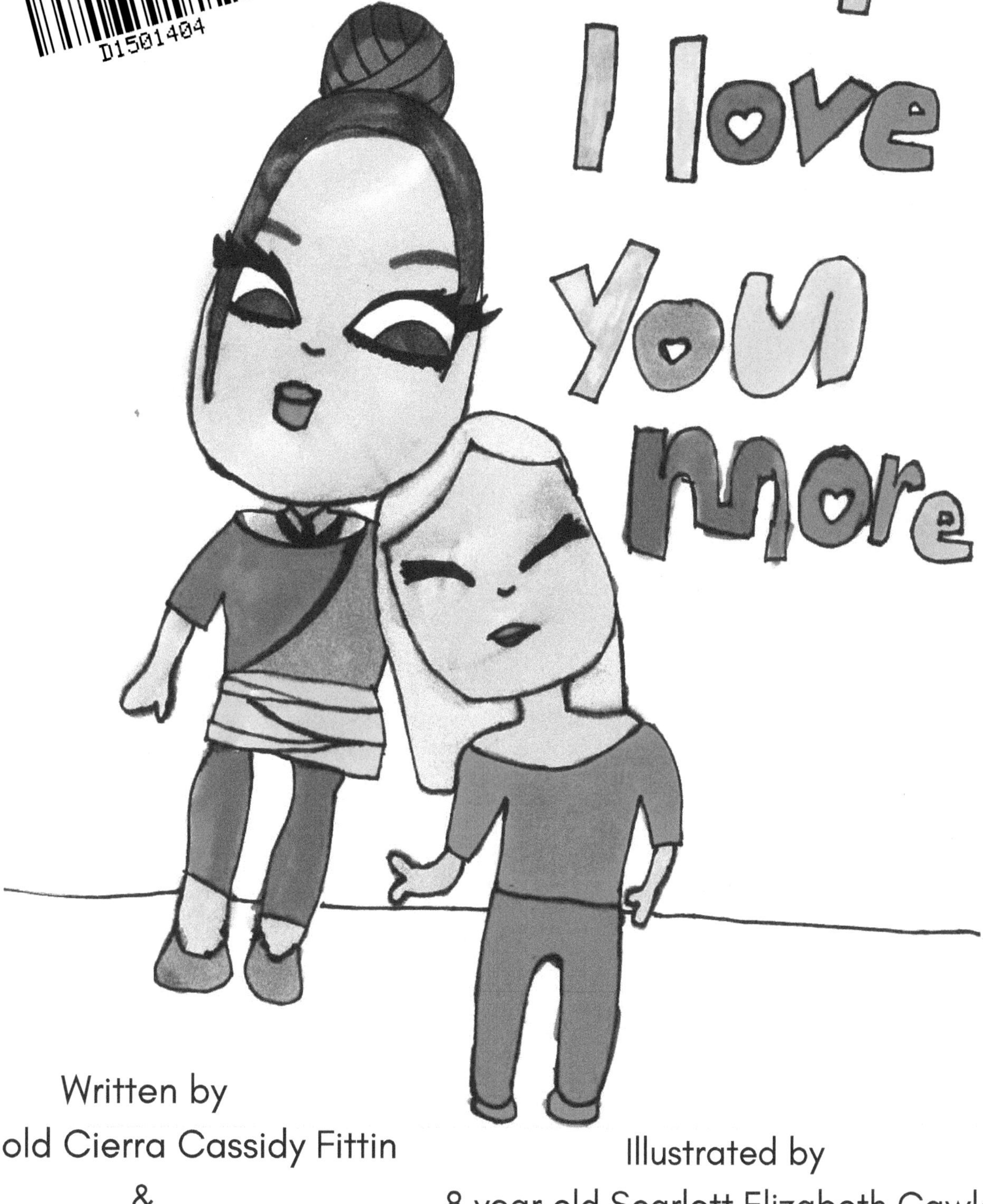

Written by
7 year old Cierra Cassidy Fittin
&
her mom Sheree Severini-Fittin

Illustrated by
8 year old Scarlett Elizabeth Cawley

I dreamed of you my entire life. While waiting for you I have loved so much. But there is no love that compares to my love for you.

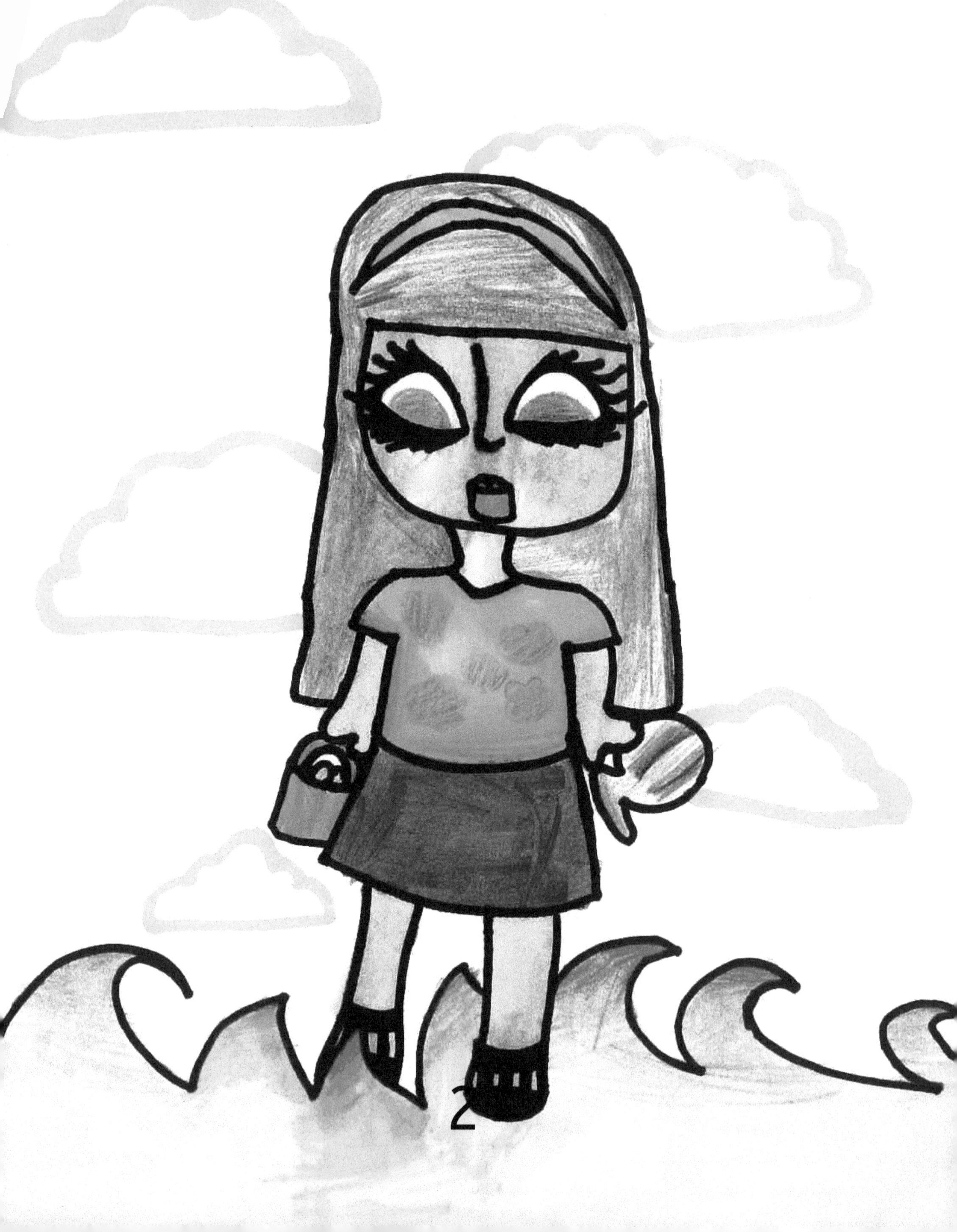

I love walks on the sandy beach in the early mornings. Searching for seashells and listing to the waves crash on the sand.

But I love you more...

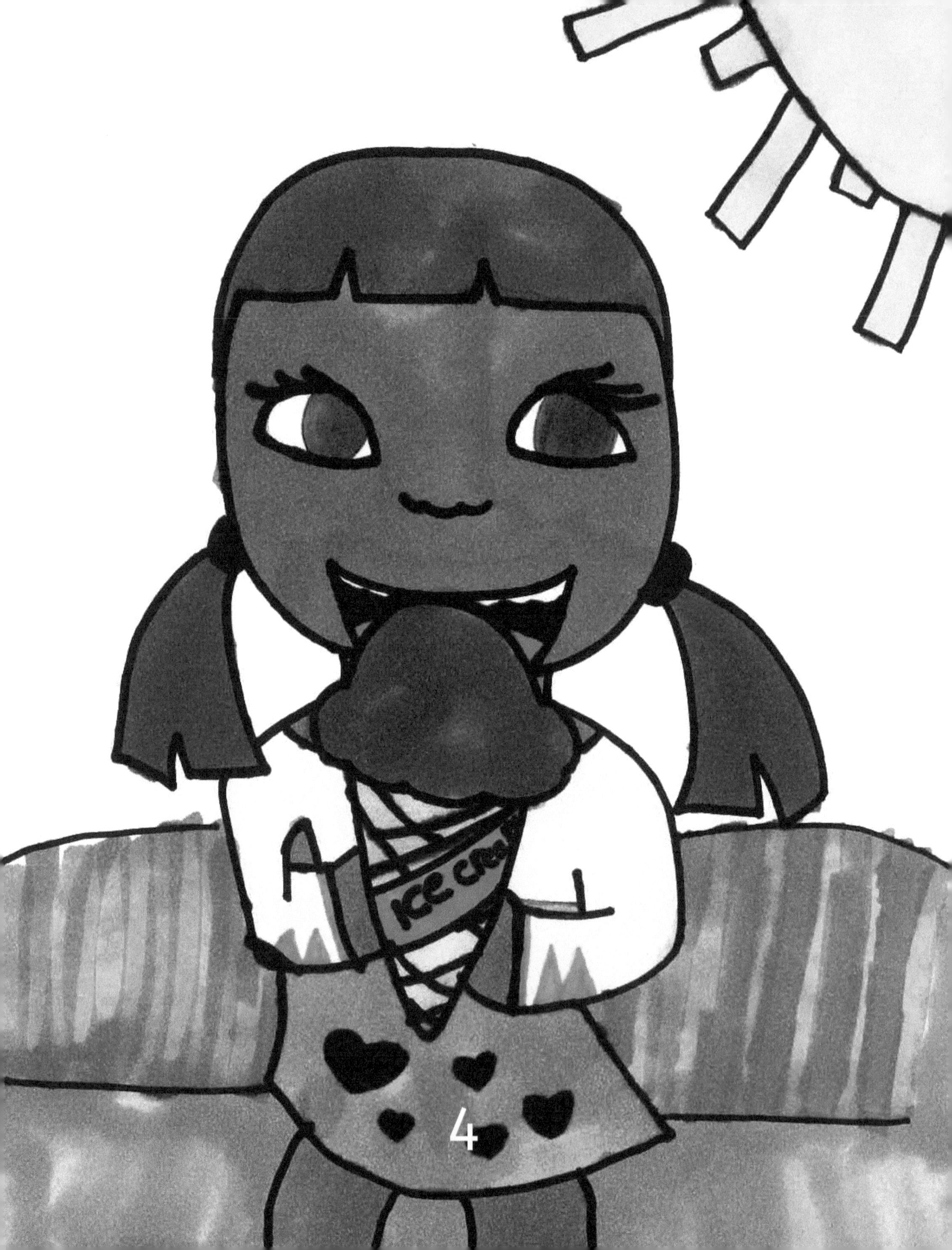
ICE CRE

I love licking ice cream in a large cone on a hot sunny day with the ice cream melting down my hand.

But I love you more...

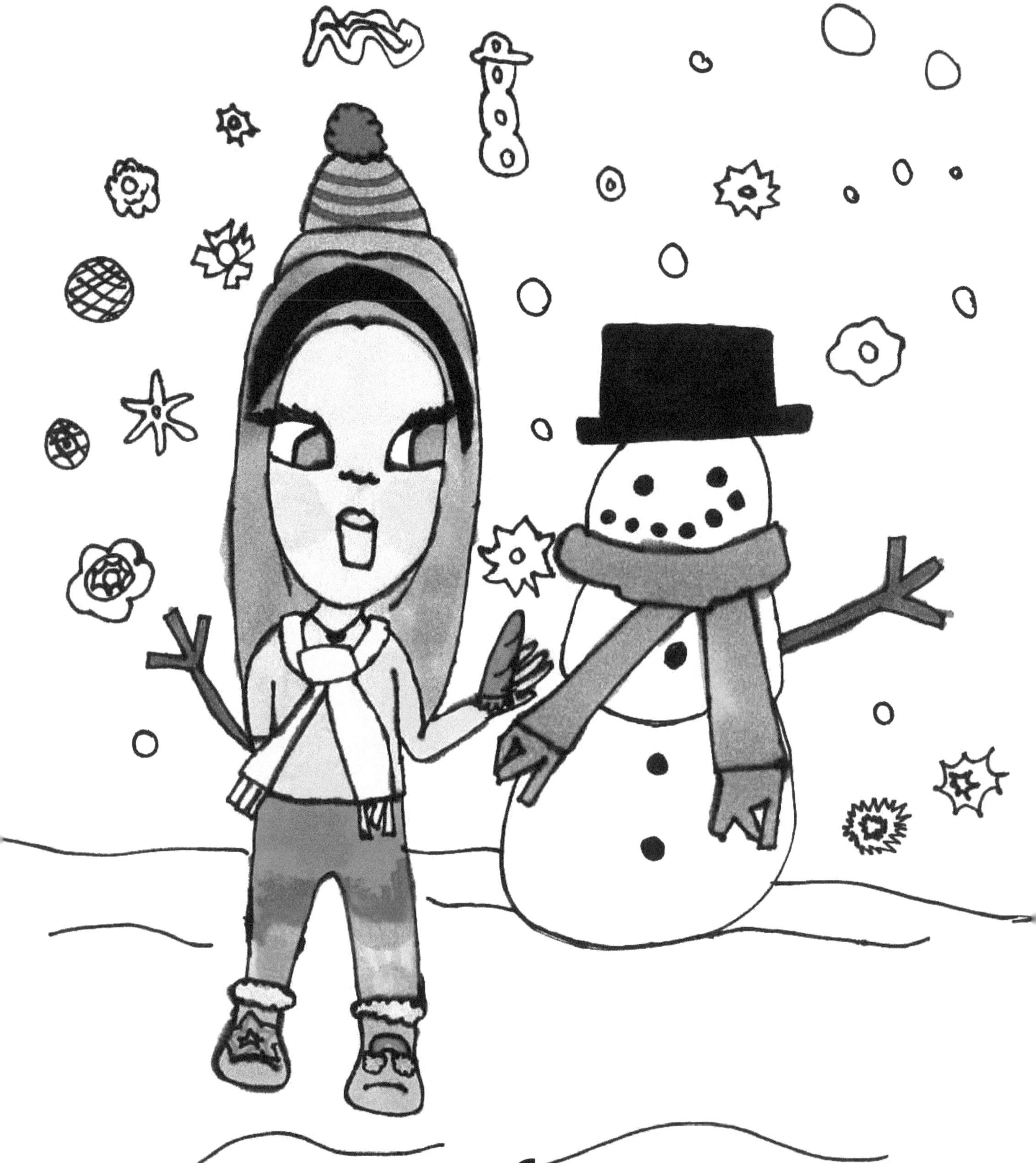

I love playing in the snow making snow angels and building a snow man after a fresh snow has fallen.

But I love you more...

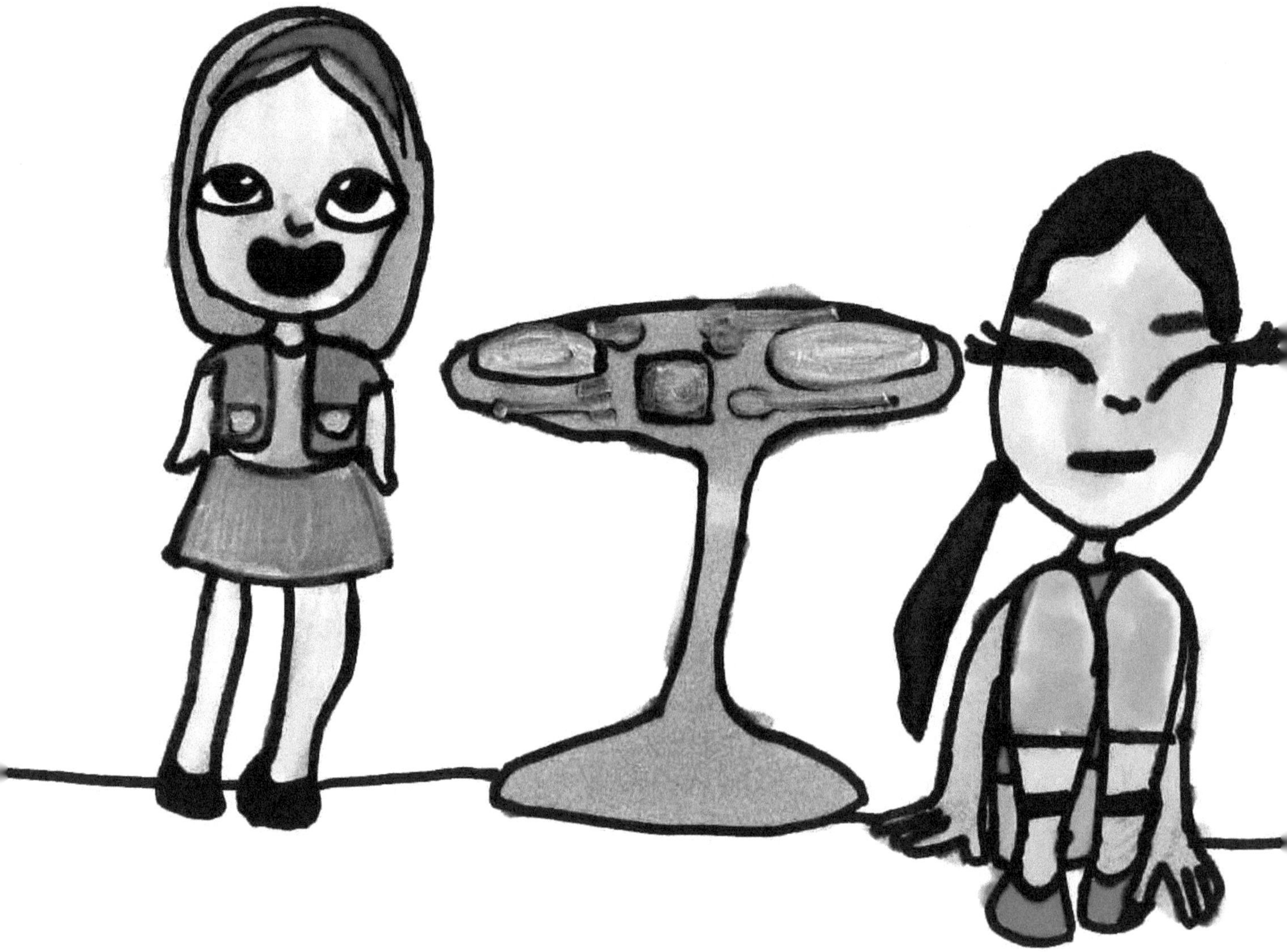

I love playing hide and seek. The way you hide under the table or blanket. And when I start looking for you, you yell out "here I am".

But I love you more...

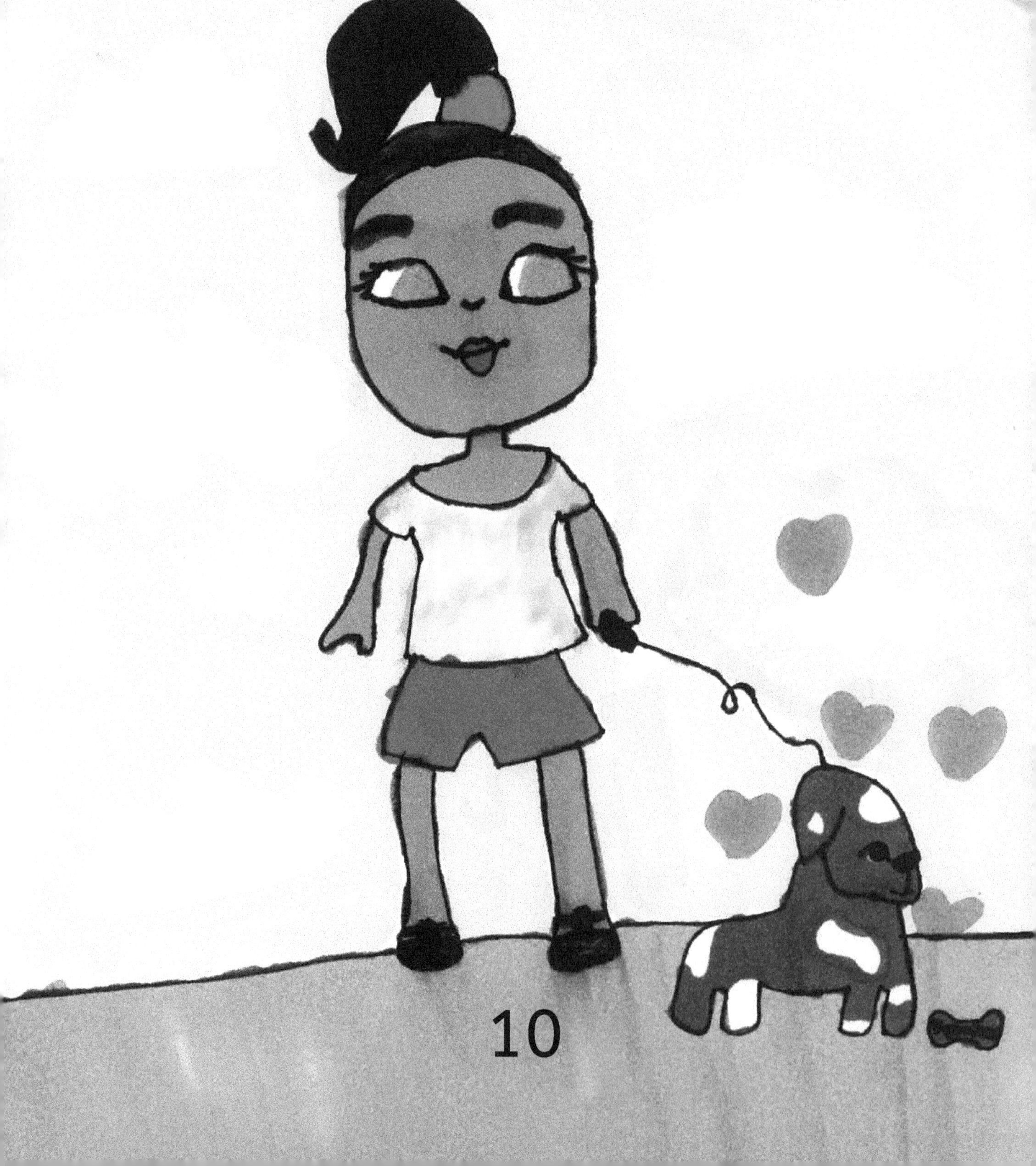

I love teaching my dog tricks, playing catch with her, tug of war and taking her for long walks.

But I love you more...

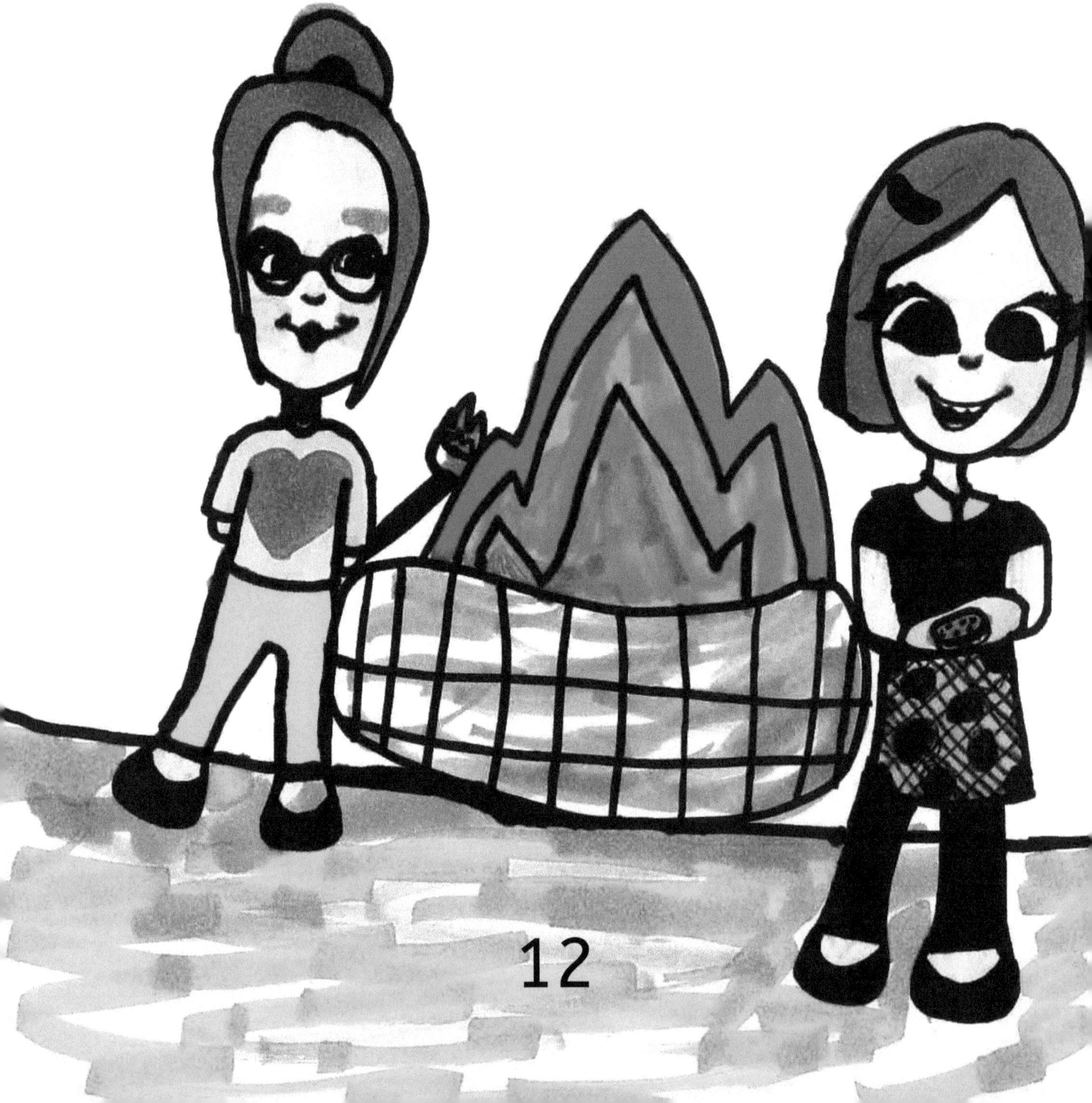

I love toasting marshmallows over a crackling fire to the point where the marshmallow catches fire and is just about to fall into the fire.

But I love you more...

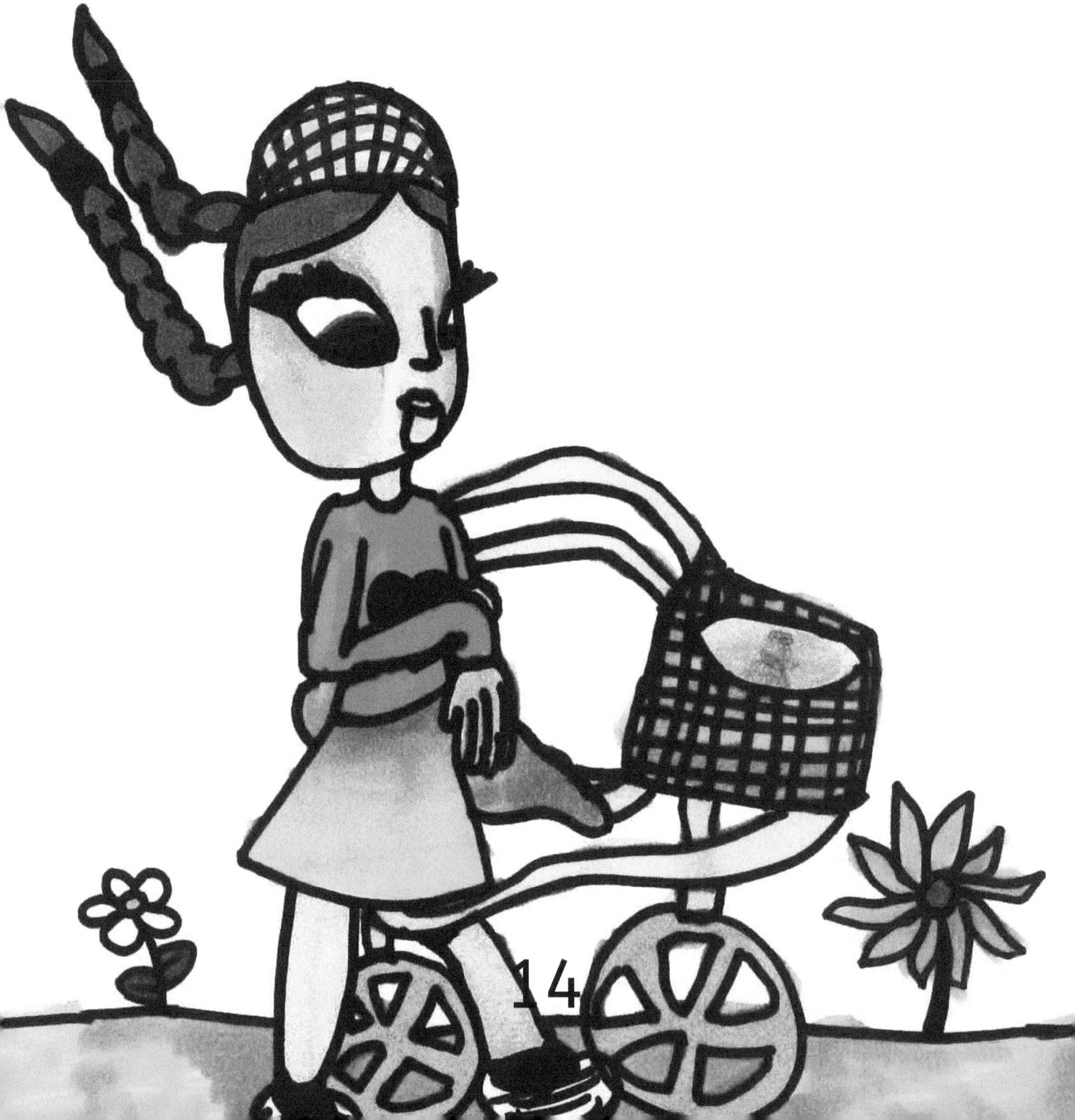

I love riding my bicycle
and feeling the wind
blow through my hair.
But I love you more...

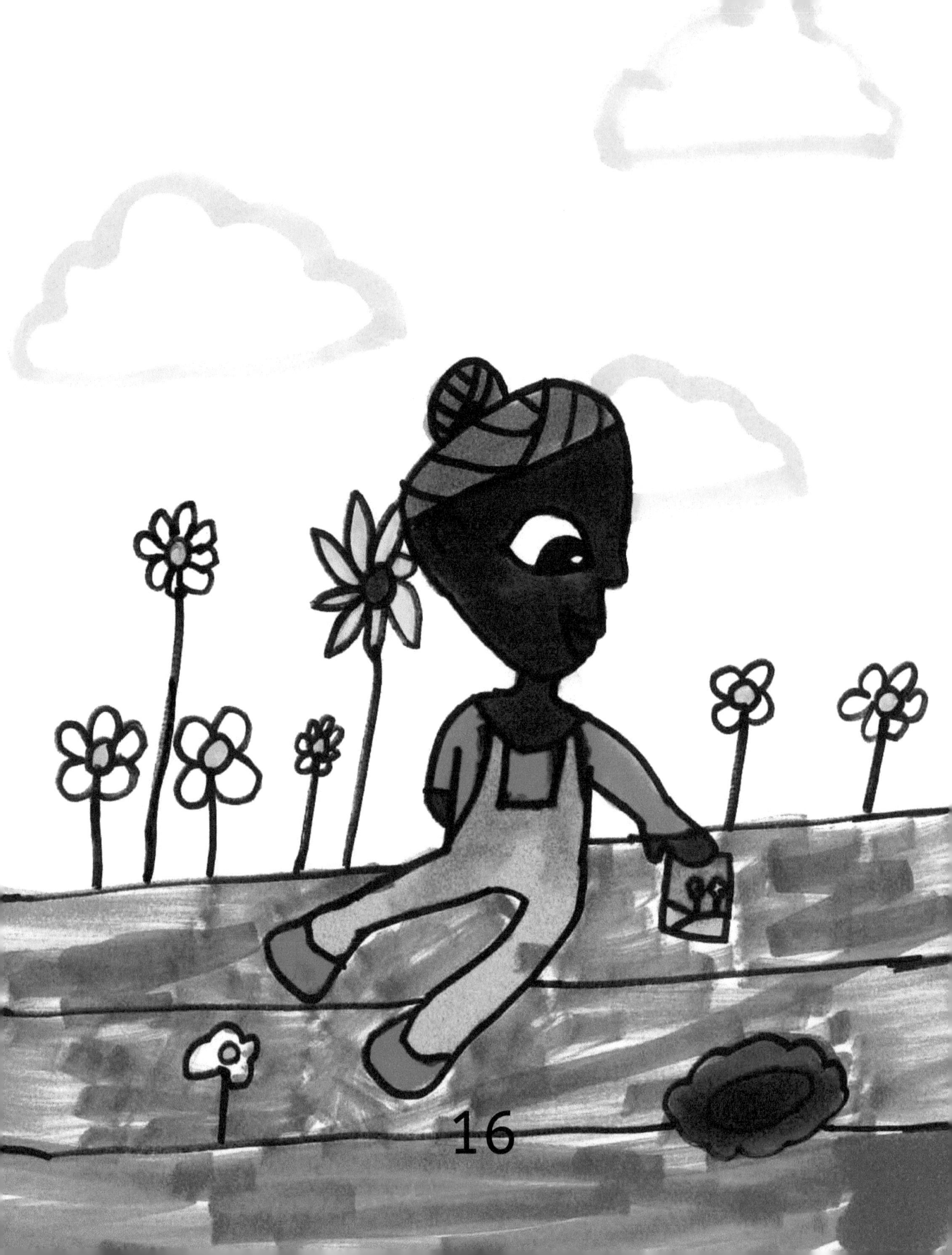

I love planting in my garden, watering the seeds and watching the flowers bloom day after day.

But I love you more...

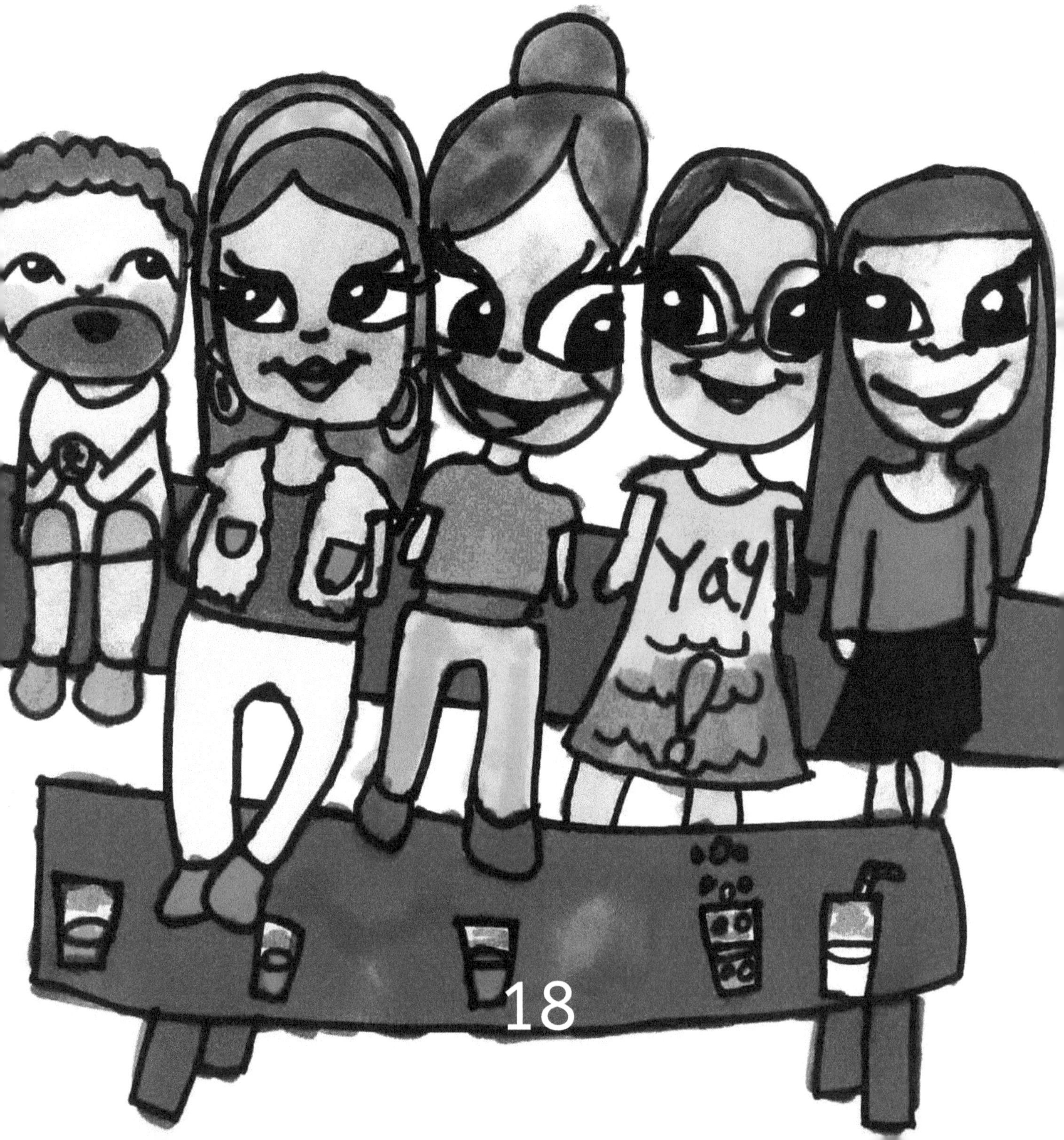
YAY
!

I love sitting with good friends enjoying a drink, remembering stories and laughing with them so hard that we begin to cry. But I love you more...

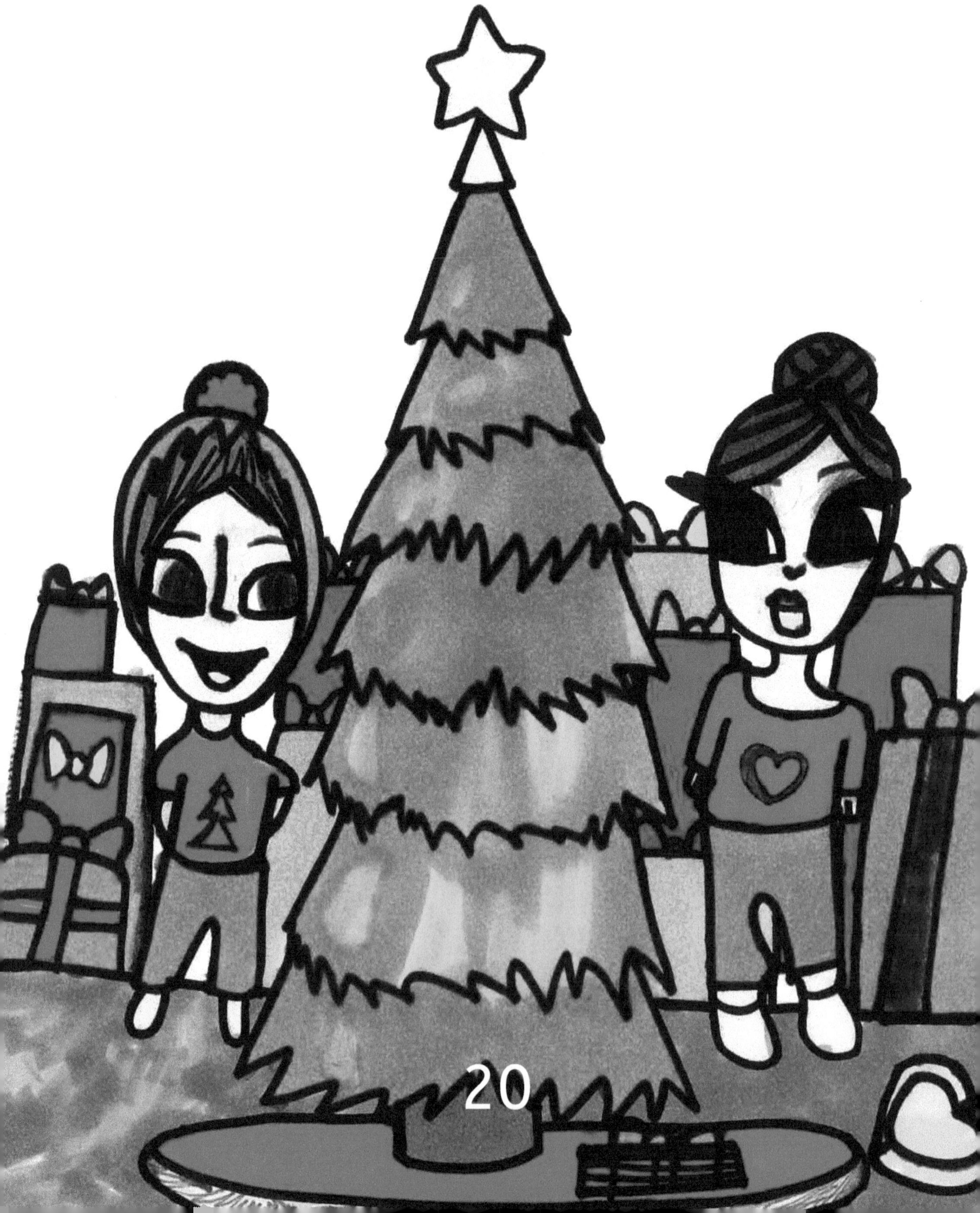

I love Christmas morning, seeing all the presents under the tree just waiting to be unwrapped.

But I love you more...

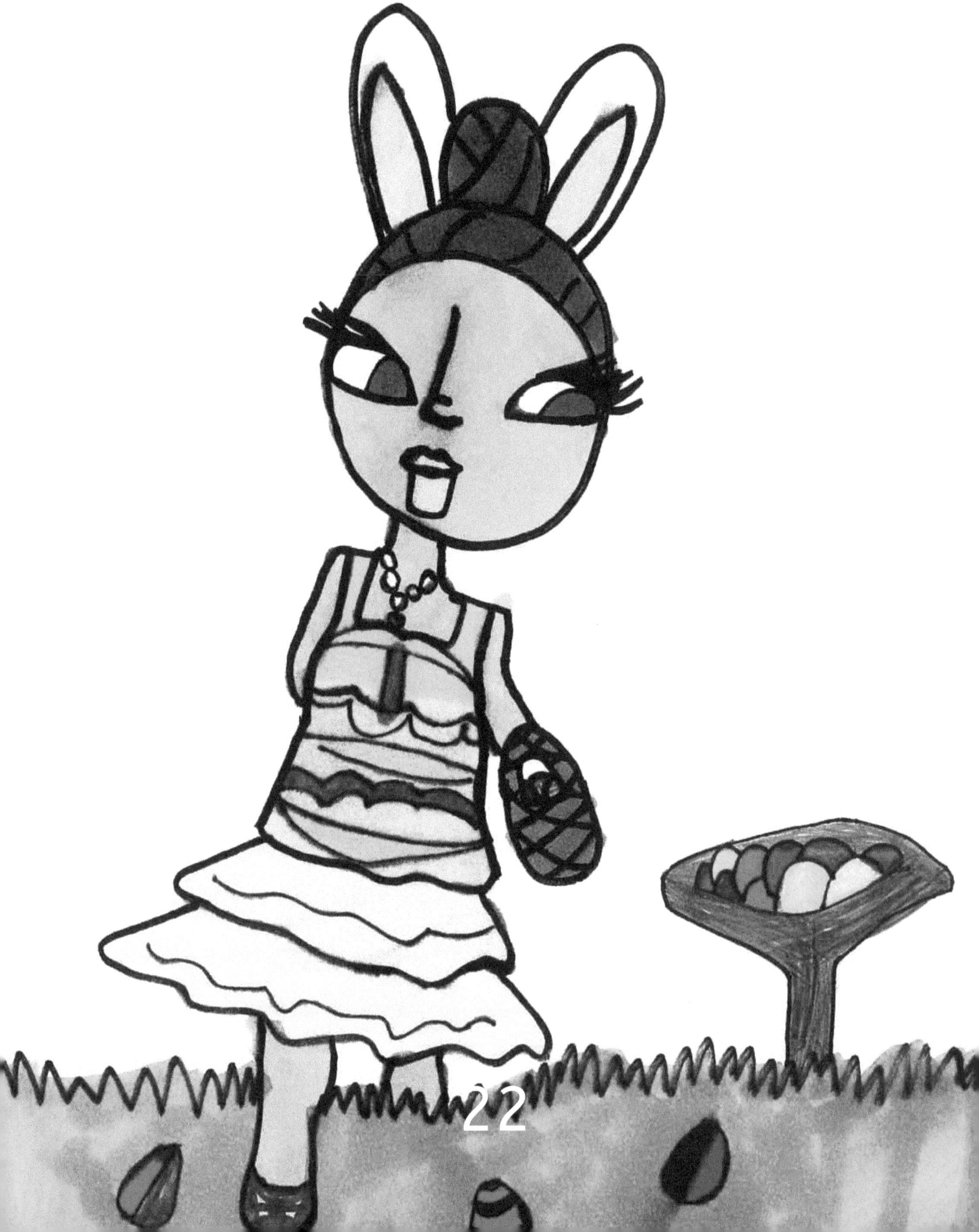

I love Easter morning
when all the colorful
eggs have been hidden
by the easter bunny
just waiting to be
found.

But I love you more...

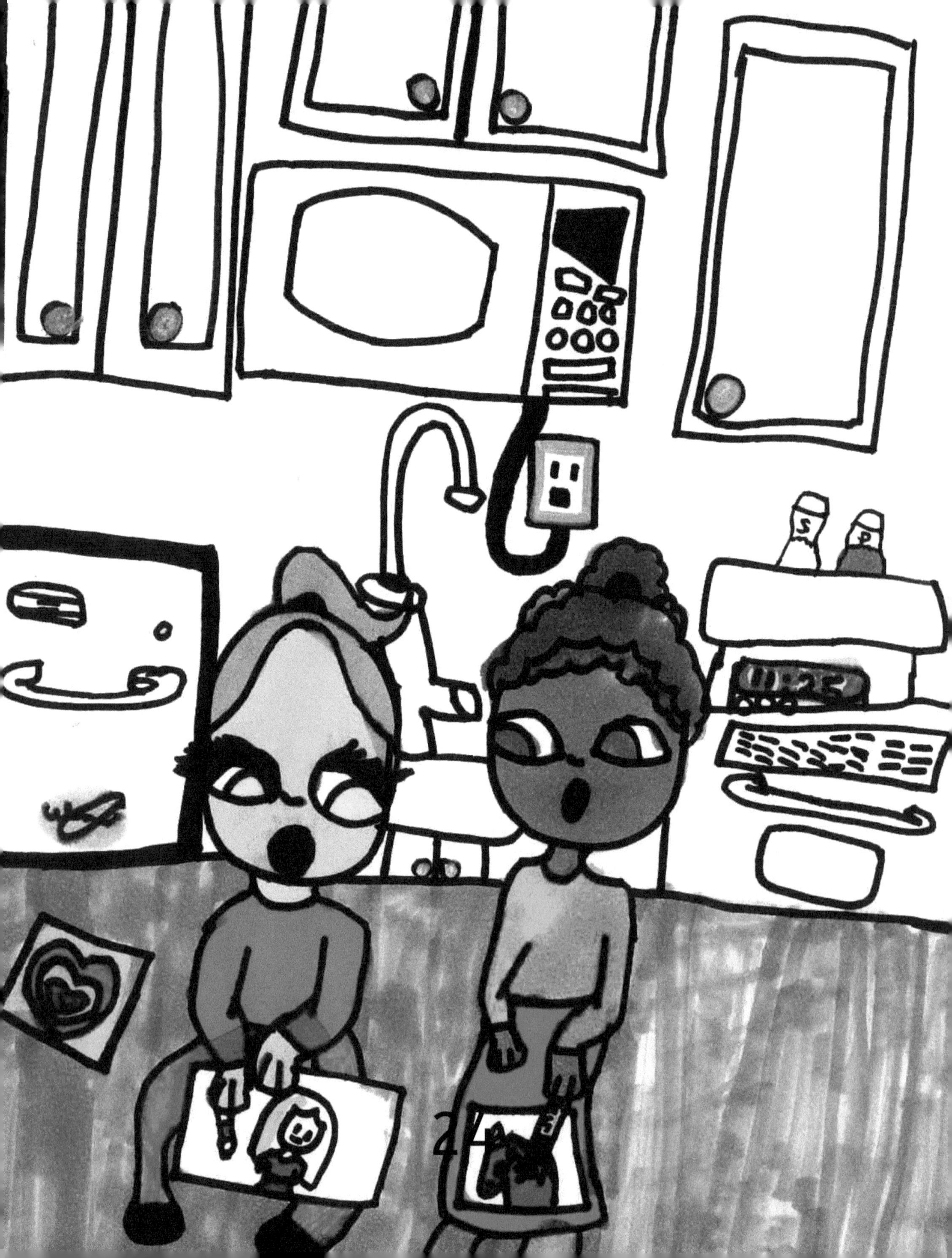
S
P

I love sitting around the kitchen, coloring and crafting with family and friends.

But I love you more...

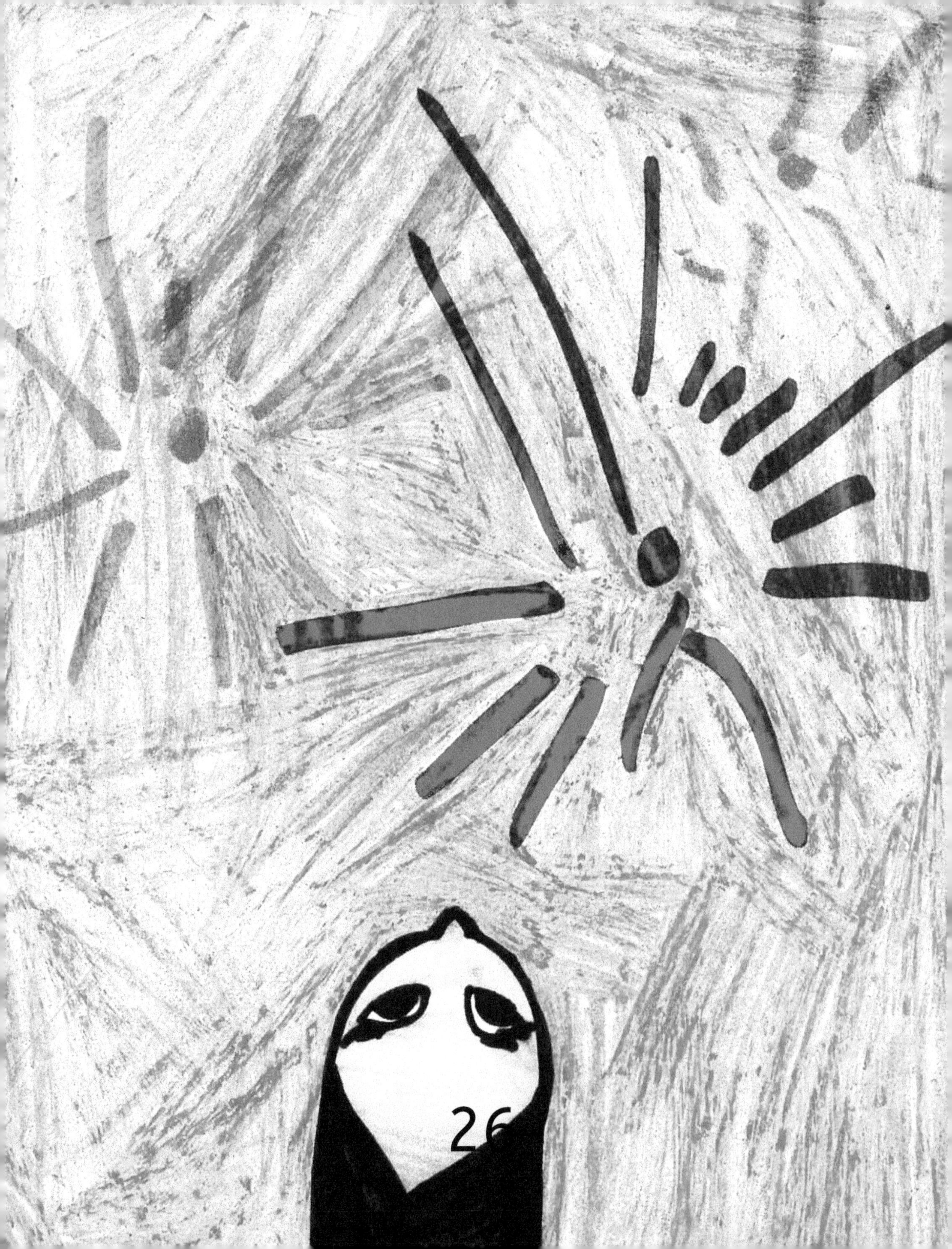

I love a clear blue
night watching
fireworks explode in
the sky. Listening to
the crackle and booms
each one makes. And
the way the colors
light up the night sky.
But I love you more...

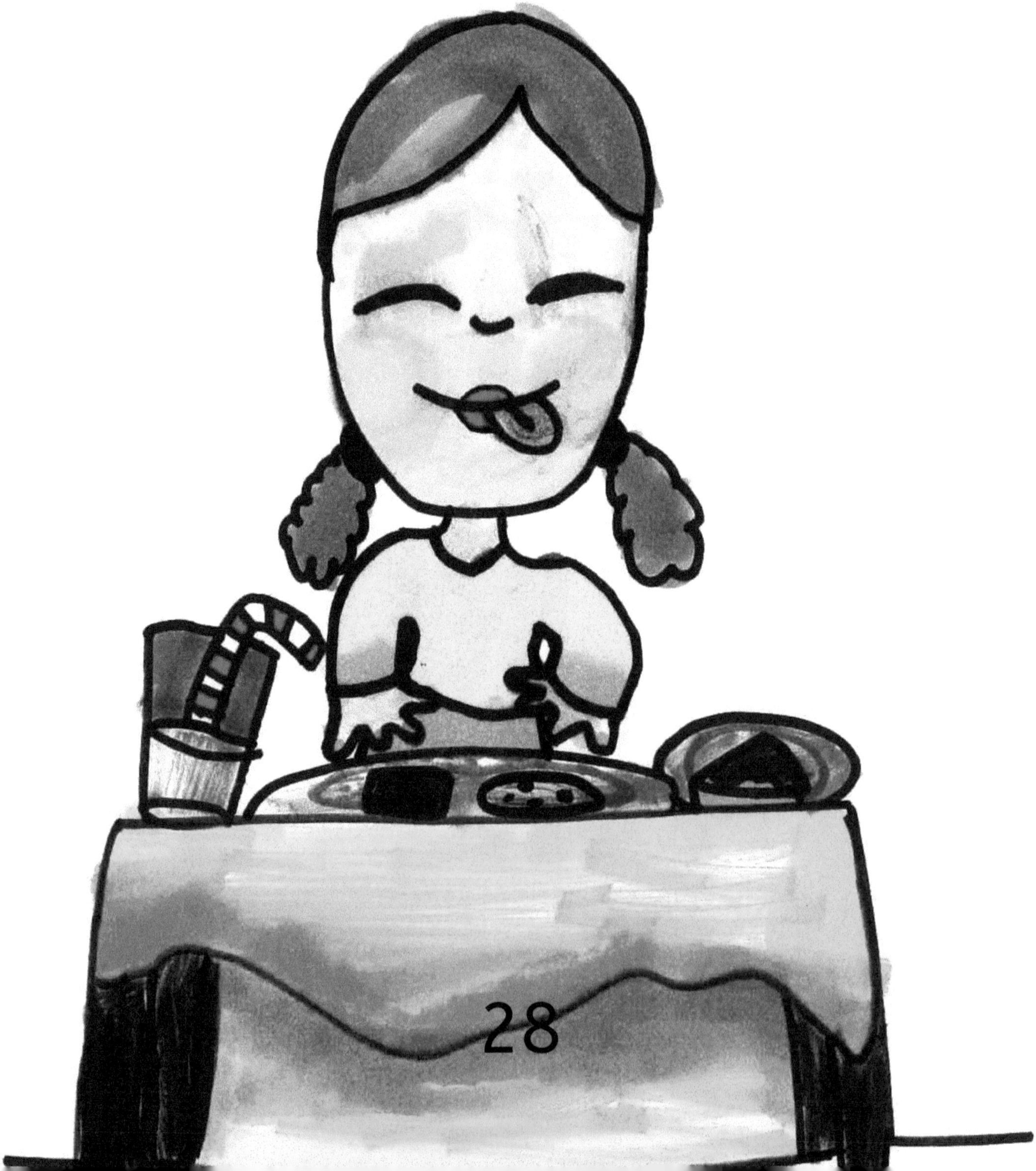

I love the scent of cookies, cakes and brownies baking in the oven. Then sitting down to enjoy them with a large glass of milk.

But I love you more...

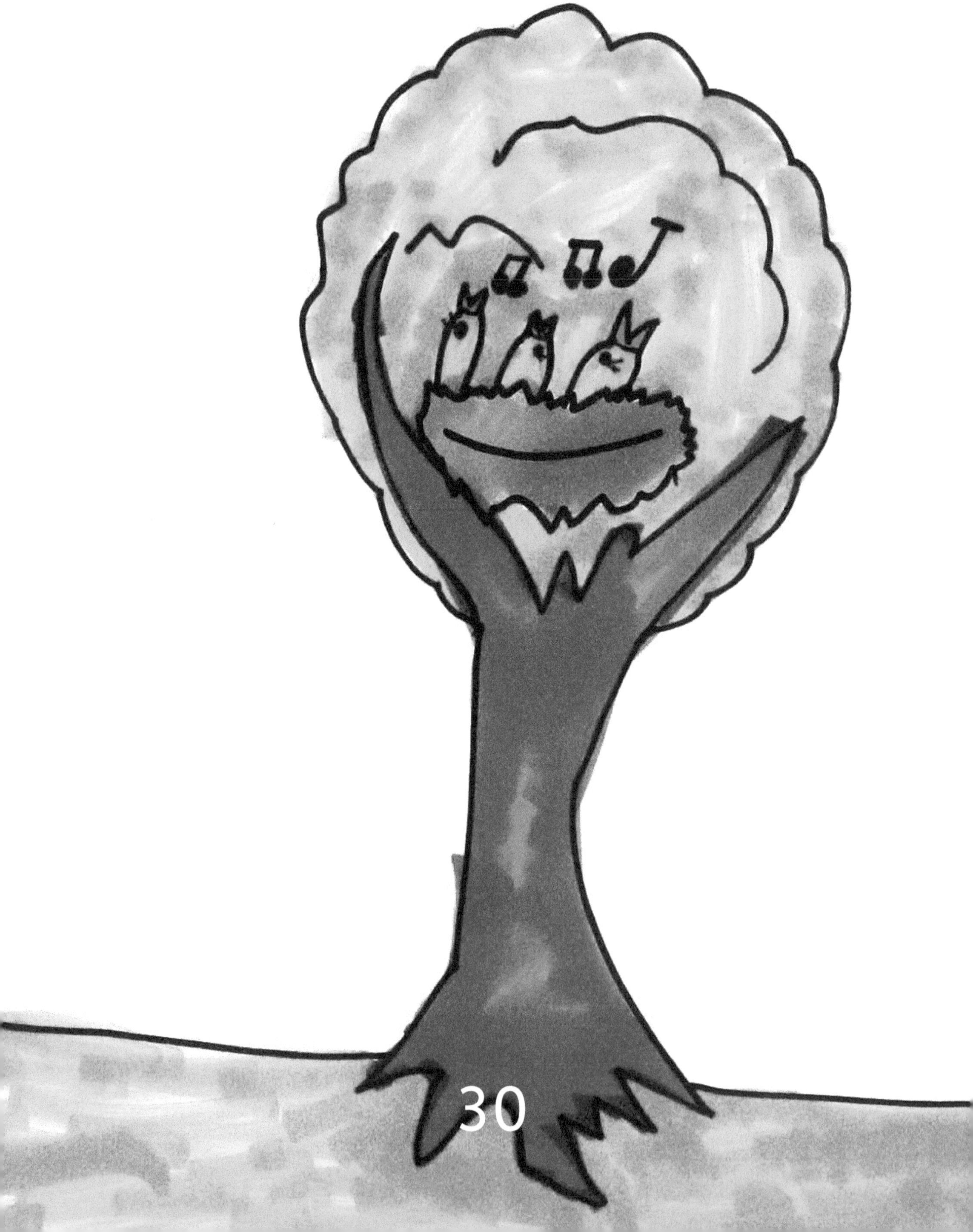

I love listening to the
sounds of birds
chirping singing their
songs.

But I love you more...

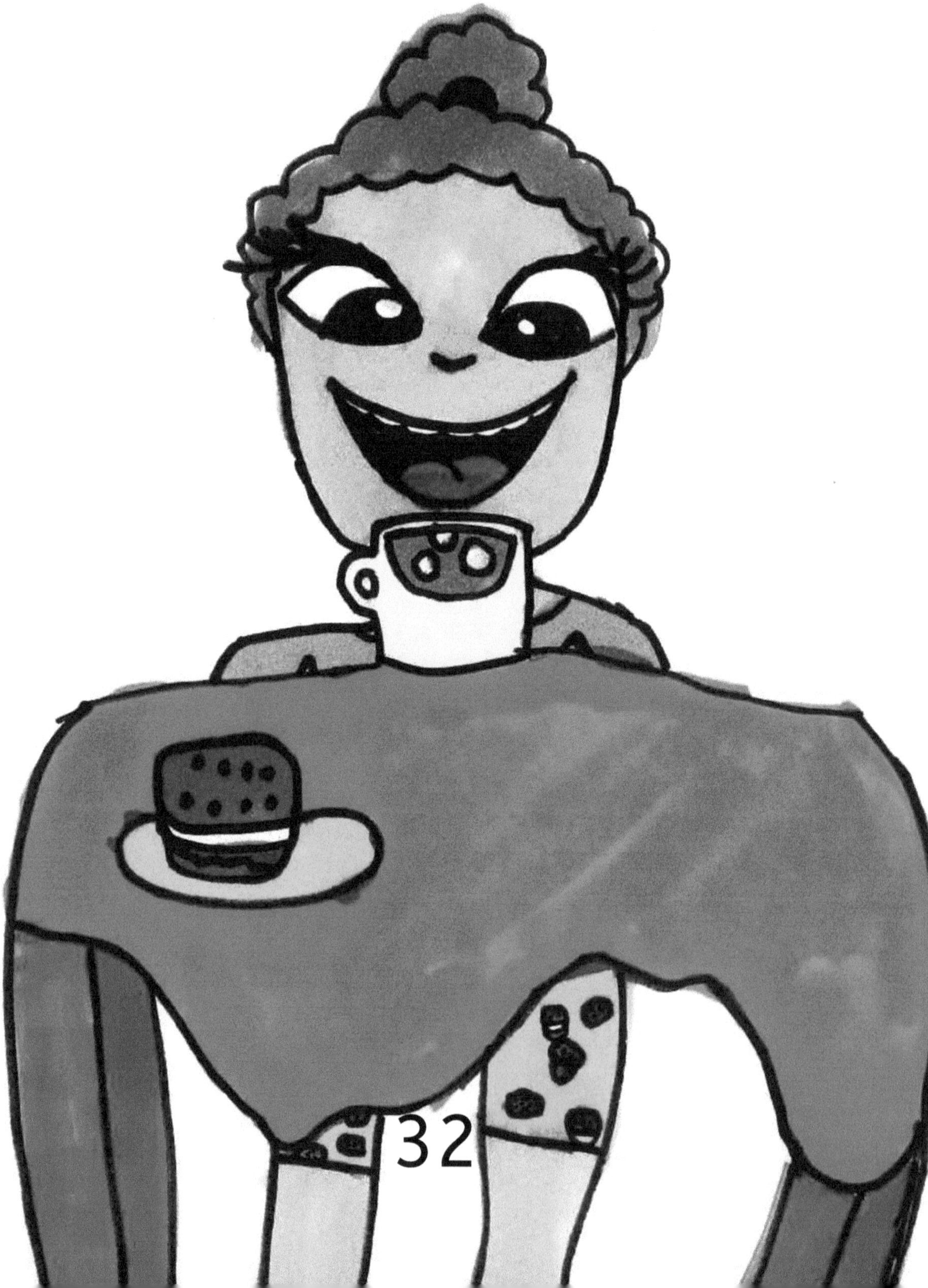

I love cupping my hands around a warm mug of hot cocoa and sipping it while the marshmallows melt on top.

But I love you more...

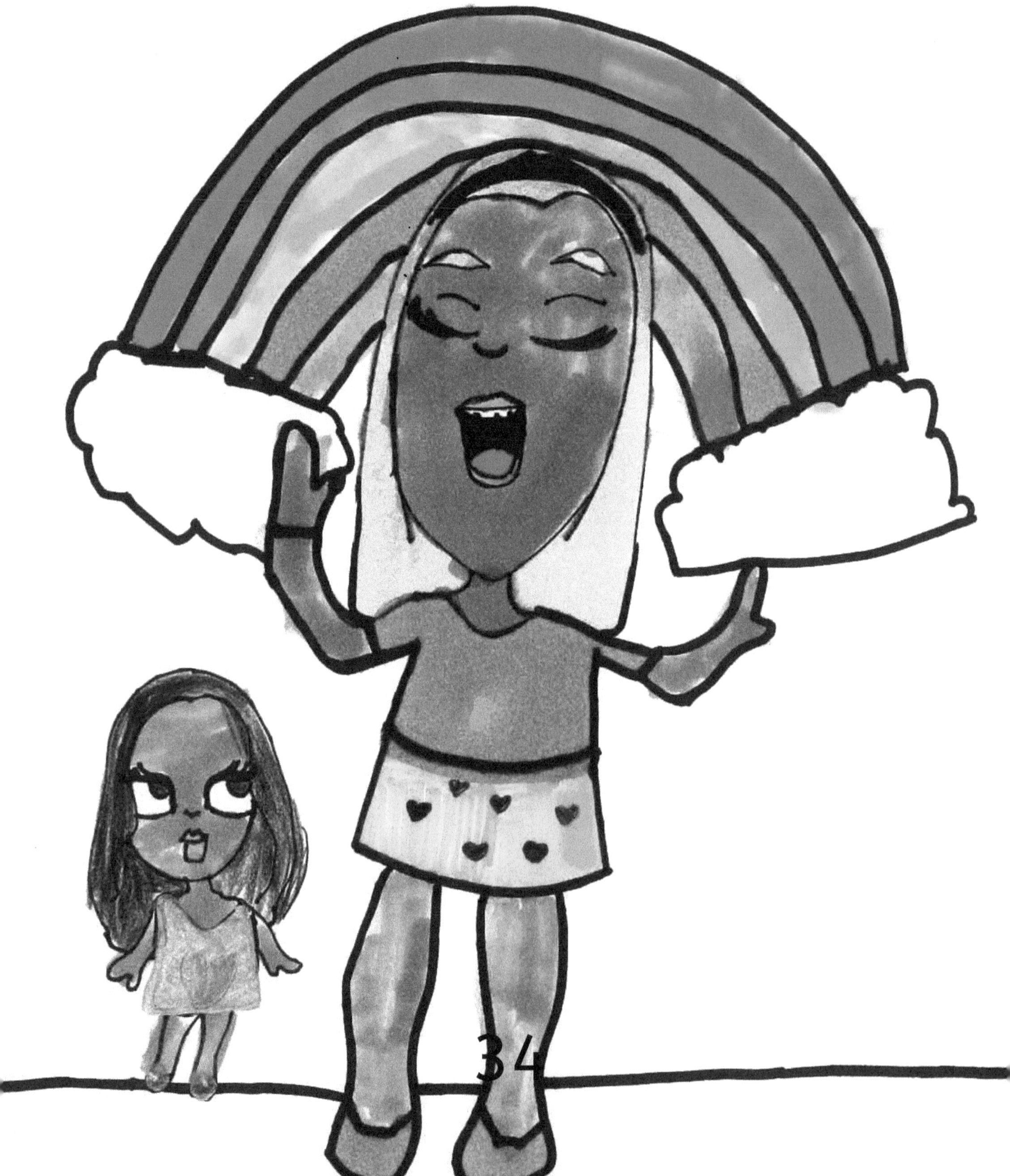

I love singing songs
like "somewhere over
the rainbow".
But I love you more...

36

I love sitting in a warm and dry place watching a rainstorm roll in. Catching glimpses of lightning off from a distance and hearing thunder drumming through the skies.

But I love you more...

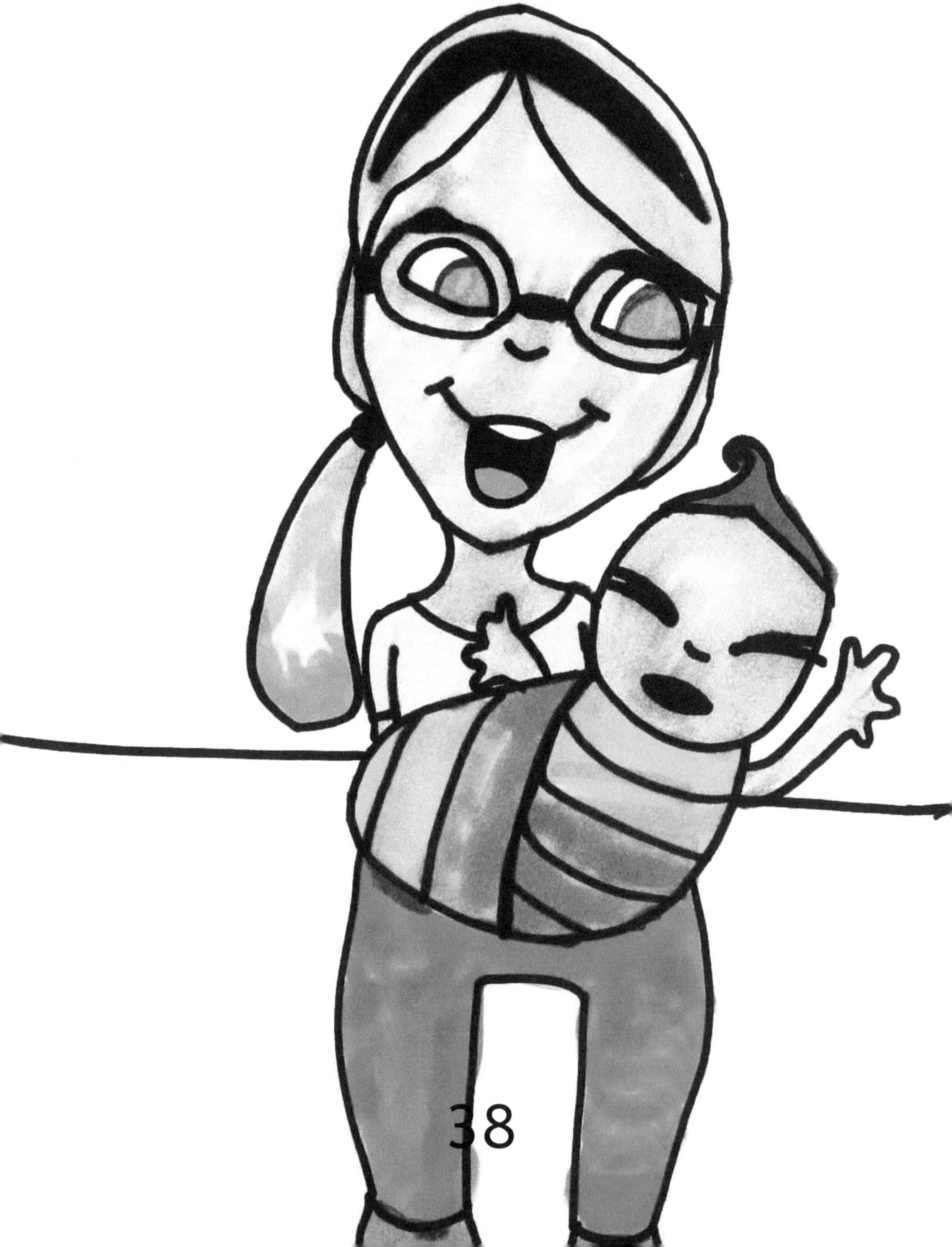

I love holding you in my arms, feeling the warmth of your skin, and listening to your heartbeat.

But I love you more...

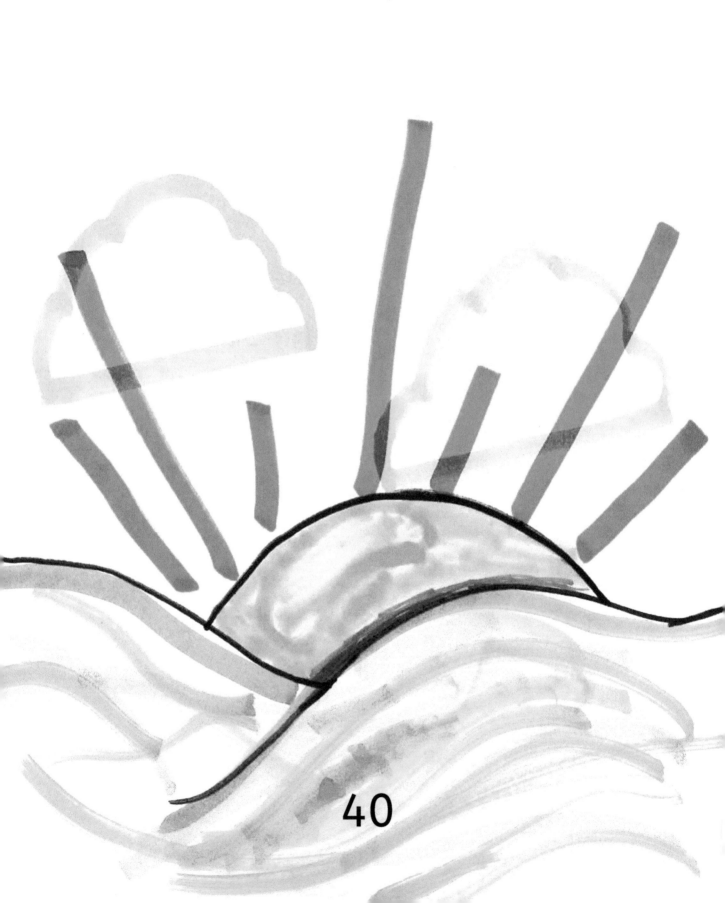

40

I love catching a sun rise over the ocean and seeing that first glimpse of the orange and yellow rays that peak out above the horizon.

But I love you more...

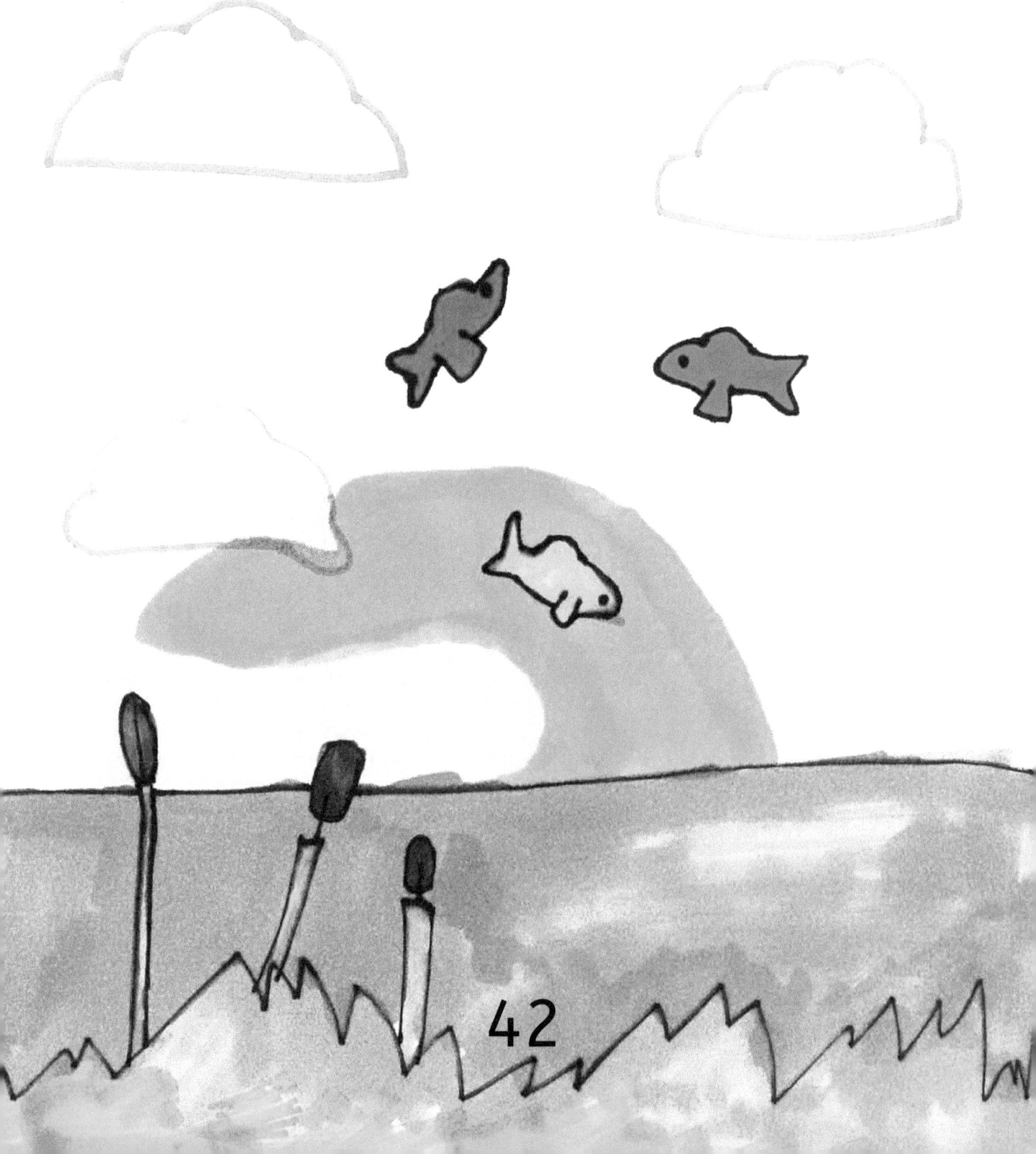

I love watching the sun set at the end of a hot day. As it dips beyond the water, I imagine the sounds of sizzling steam come off the ocean from the intense heat.

But I love you more...

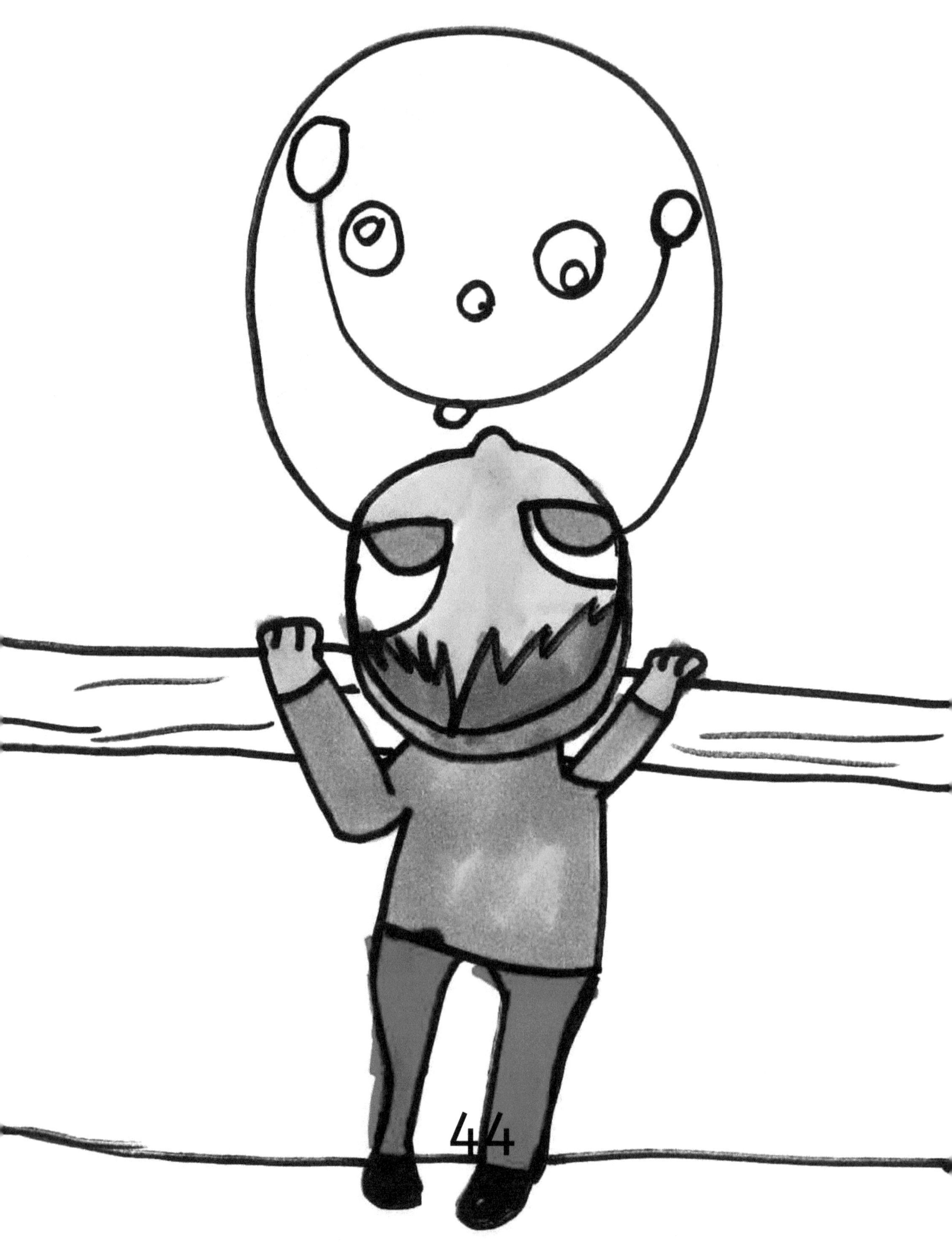

I love staring up at the moon at night and trying to picture a face on its white surface.

But I love you more...

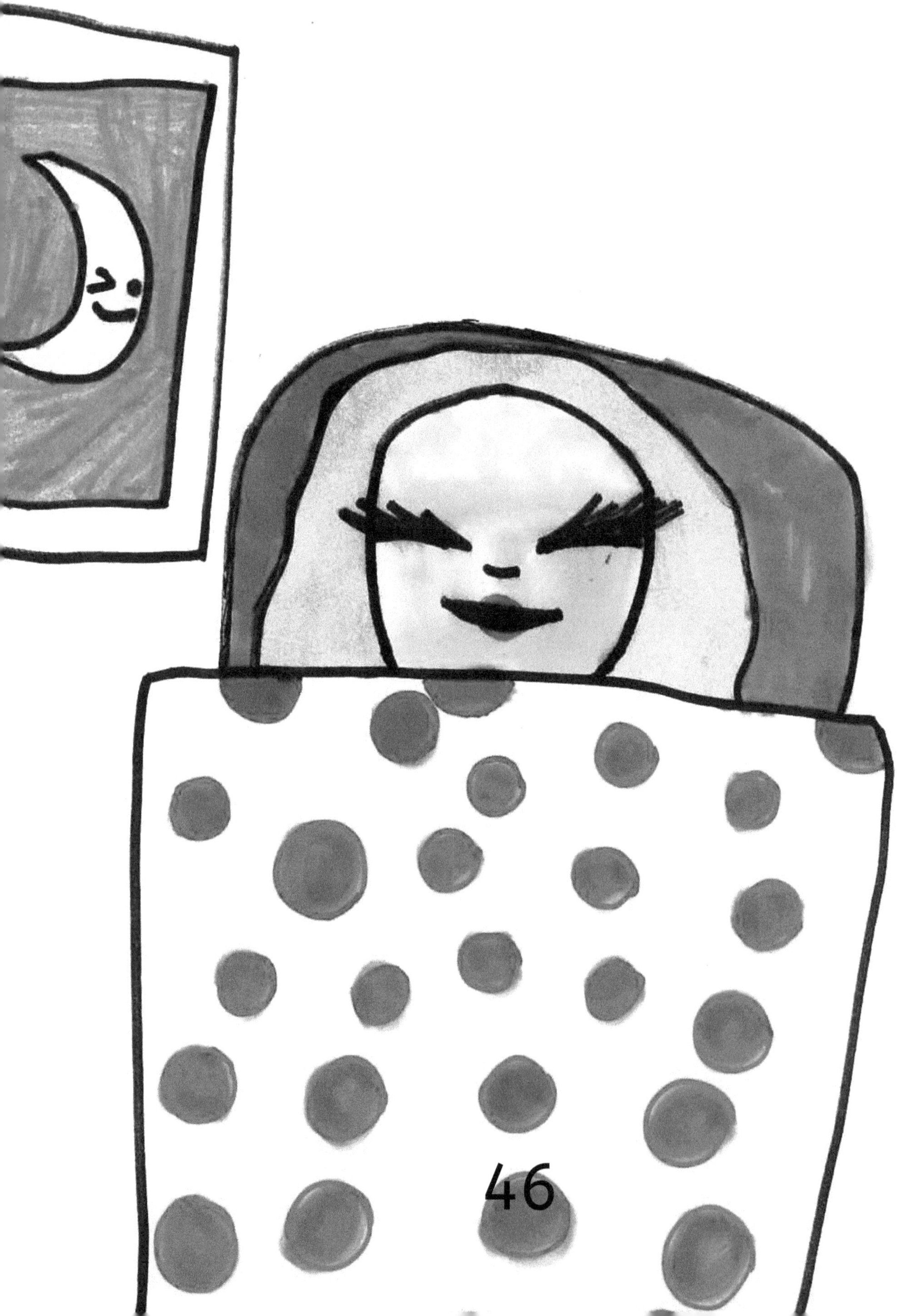

I love the sound of
your voice first thing
in the morning and
right before you place
your head on your
pillow at night.
But I love you more...

47

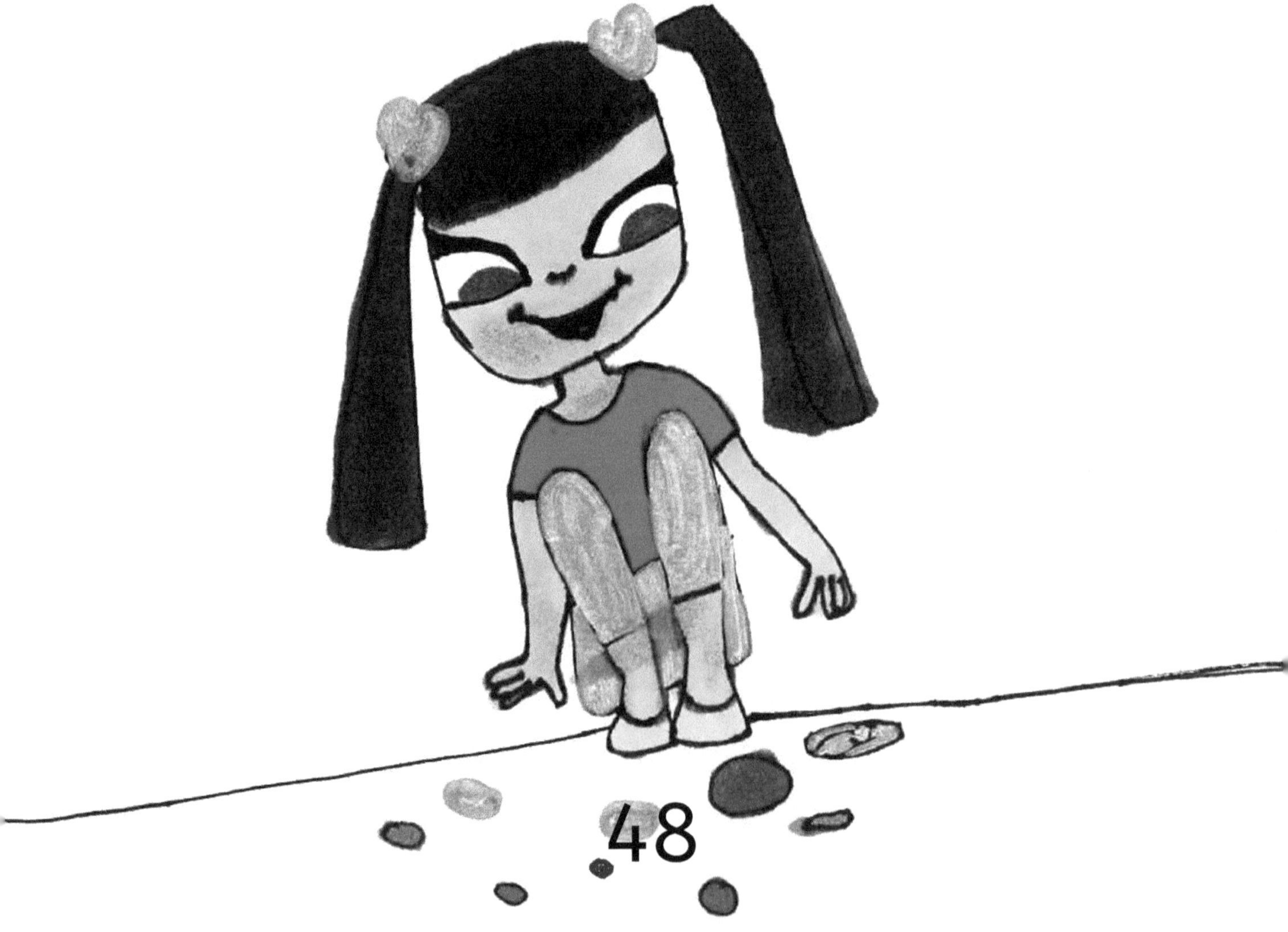

I love finding loose
change on the ground,
like pennies, nickels and
dimes. As if they were
dropped from heaven.

But I love you more...

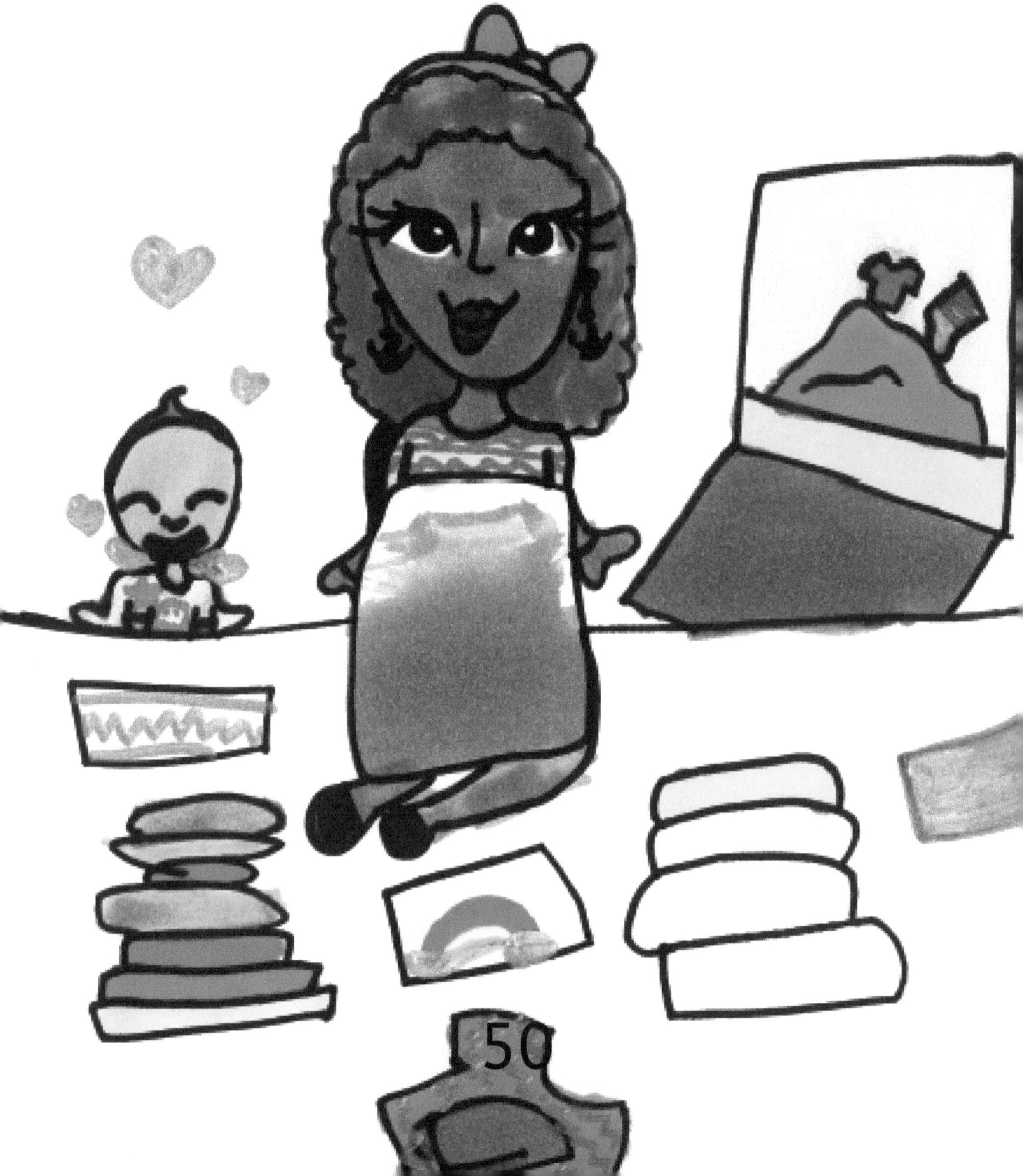

I love the fresh smell
and warm feel of
towels and sheets
coming out of the
dryer.

But I love you more...

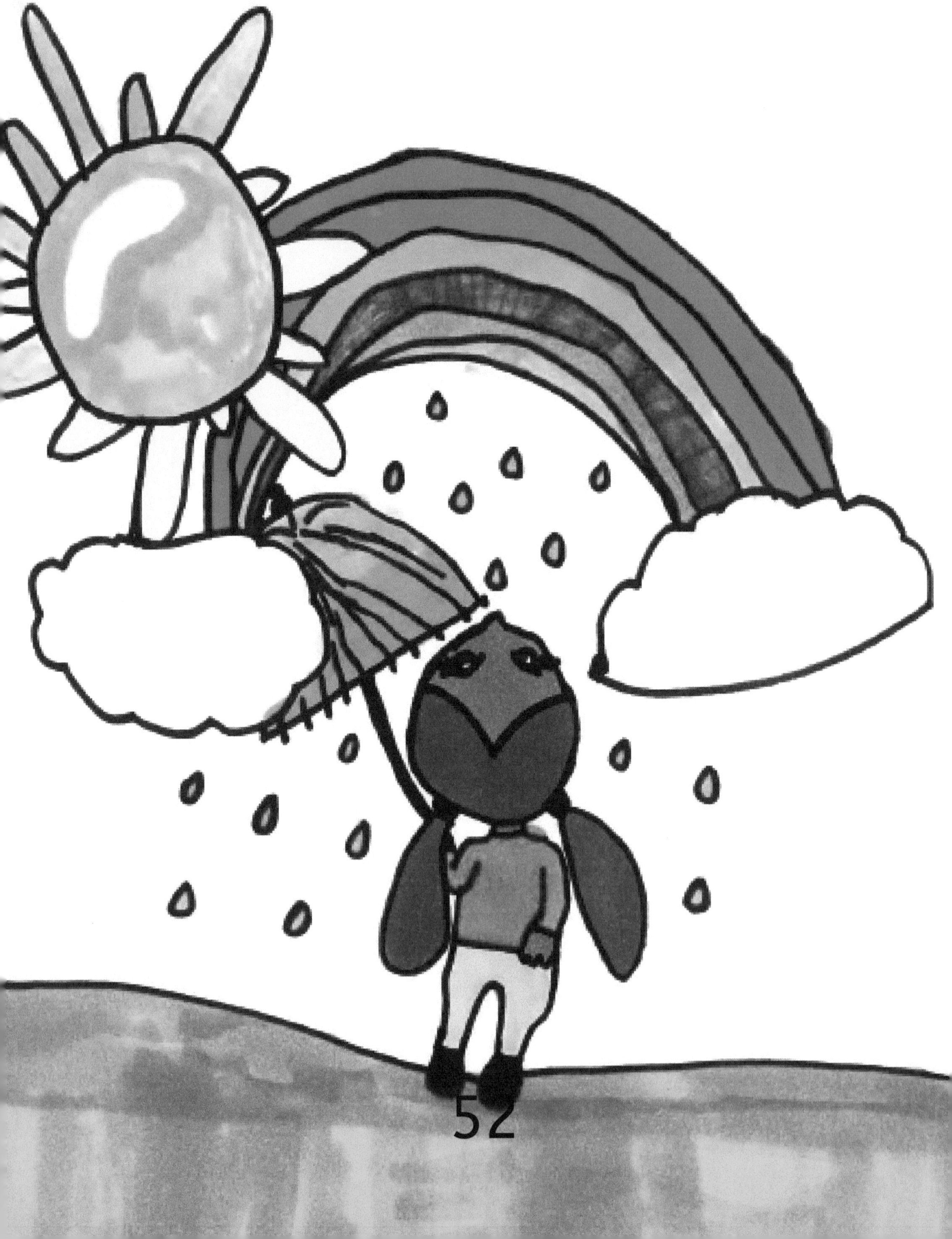

I love seeing a
rainbow high in the
sky on a sunny day
after it rains.
But I love you more...

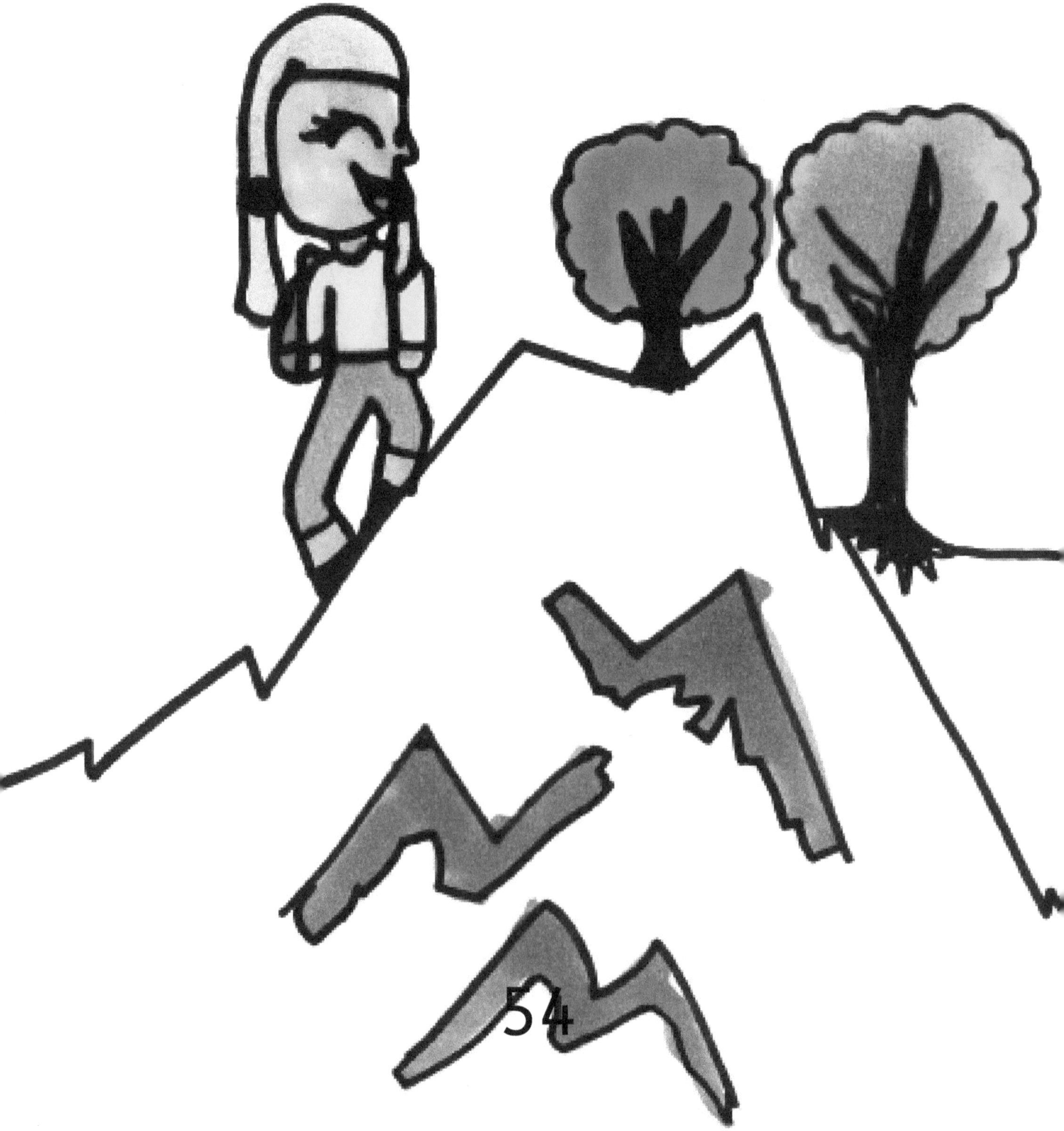

I love climbing to the top of the mountain and seeing the colorful fall trees lined below and across the fields.

But I love you more...

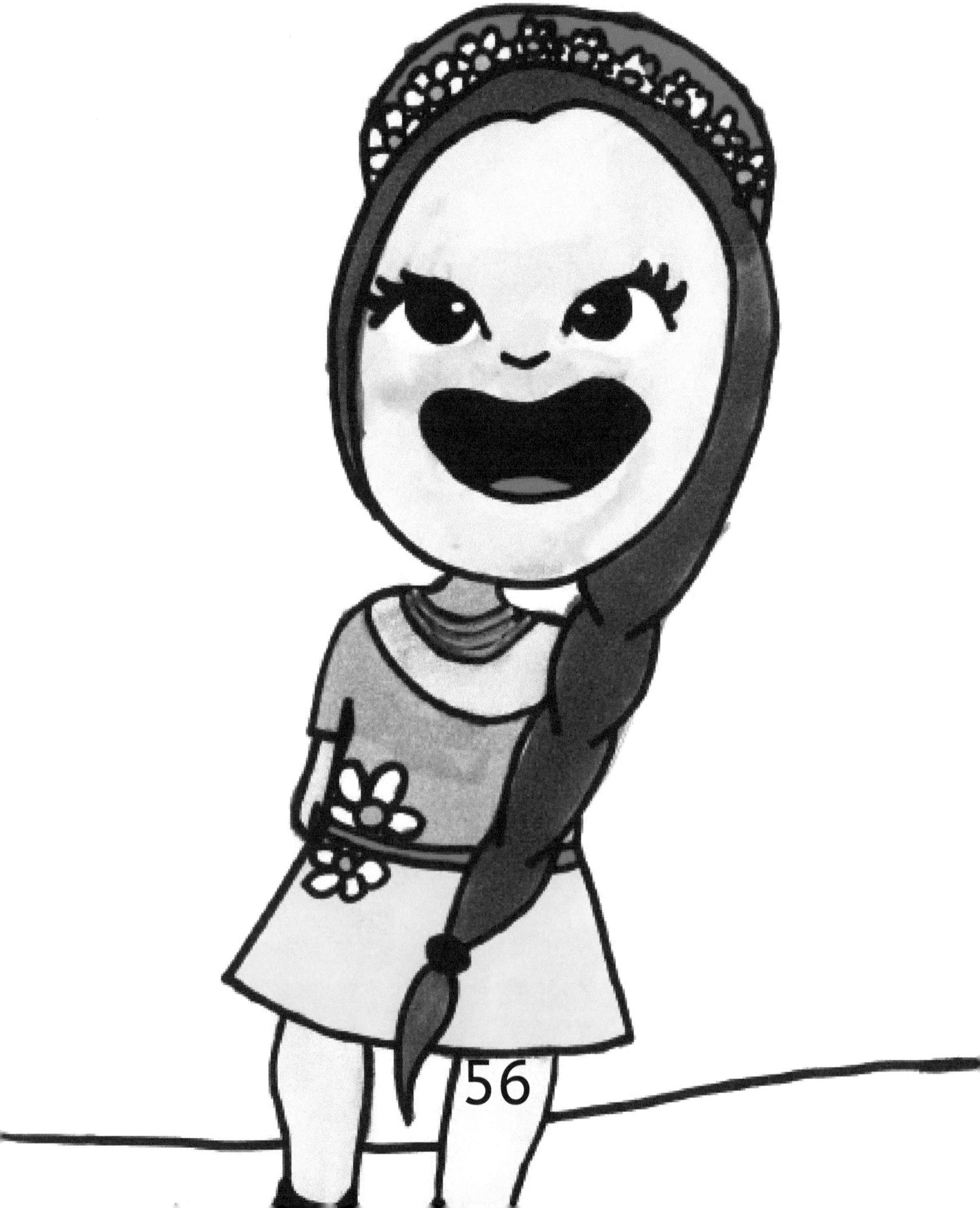

I love the way you
smile. And how your
eyes squint with
happiness.
But I love you more...

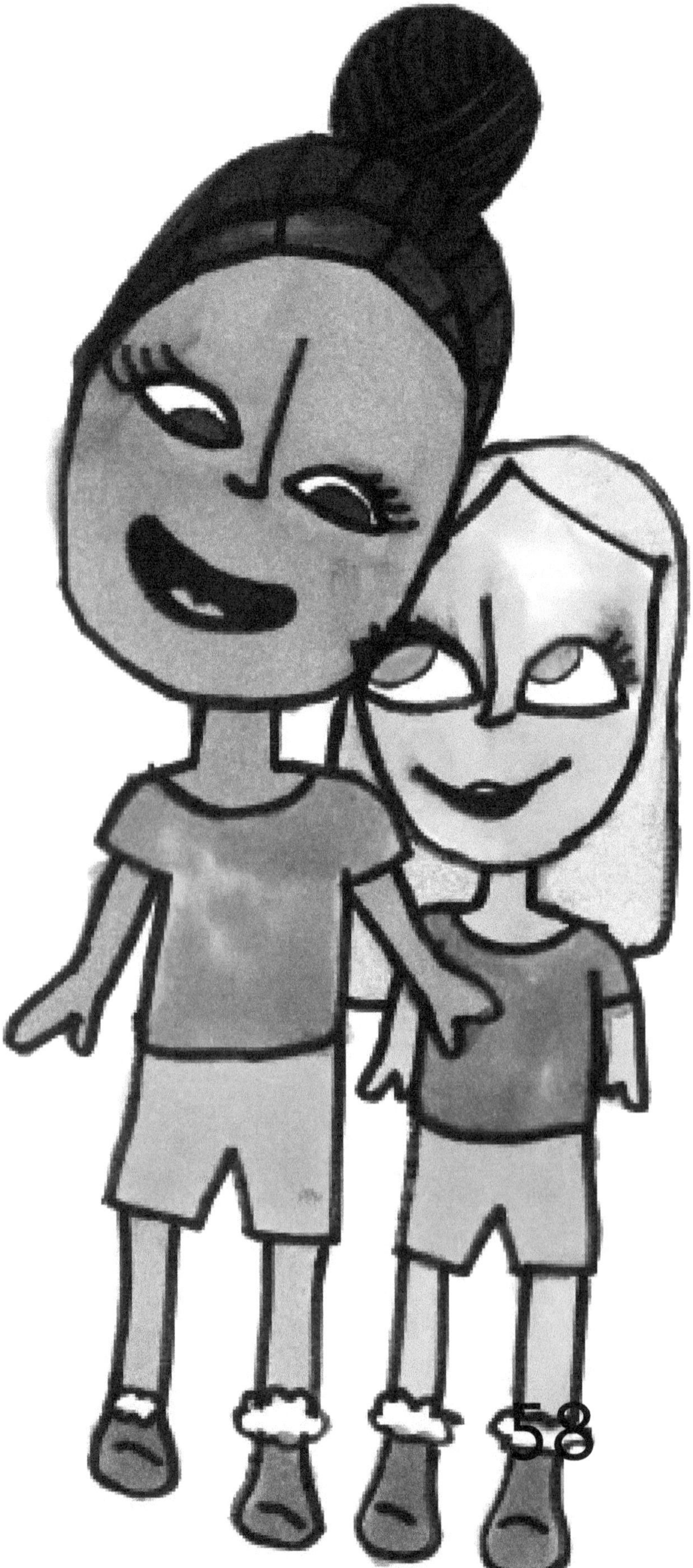

I love everything about you. The way you laugh and cry. The color of your hair and eyes. When you are angry or mad, and happy or sad. When you scream and yell or giggle and snort. I love your compassion, your kindness, your sweetness and generosity. I love how you care for others and are always offering a hand. I love your thoughts, your silence, your voice and your sighs. There isn't anything I don't love about you.

But I love you more...

ABOUT THE AUTHOR

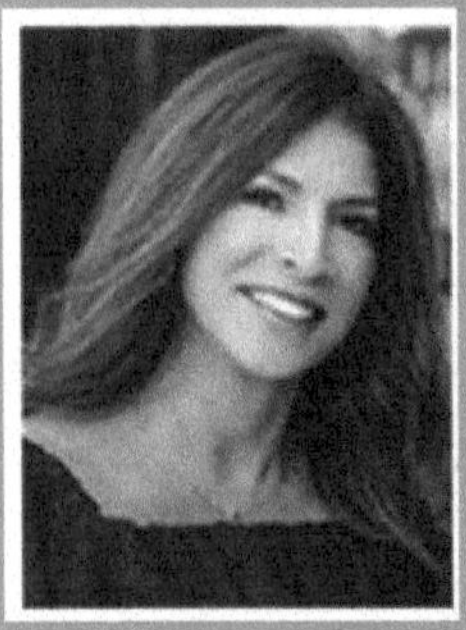

After working 25 + years in the Fashion Industry in NYC, I had my daughter at the age of 46 thanks to the miracle of science and the grace of God. I wanted to be closer to home to raise her, so I needed to reinvent myself in a new career. I am currently a Realtor helping clients buy and sell homes on the Jersey Shore (HomesbySheree@gmail.com). I have always had a passion to write, so what better way to start and test the waters than with this tribute to my daughter? I always say, you can think and dream of ideas, and that is all they will ever be, if you don't take action. Just do it already and stop thinking about it.

I hope you are able to share with your loved ones how much you truly love them with this fun and whimsical book.